The AMAZING ADVENTURES of BATMAN™

RAIN OF FEAR!

by **Brandon T. Snider**

illustrated by **Dario Brizuela**

Batman created by Bob Kane with Bill Finger

PICTURE WINDOW BOOKS
a capstone imprint

The Amazing Adventures of Batman
is published by Picture Window Books
A Capstone Imprint
1710 Roe Crest Drive
North Mankato, Minnesota 56003
www.mycapstone.com

STAR41052

Cataloging-in-Publication Data is available on the Library of Congress website.
ISBN: 978-1-5158-3981-1 (library binding)
ISBN: 978-1-5158-3986-6 (eBook PDF)

Summary: When the Scarecrow fires his fear cannon into the clouds,
Batman and Robin find themselves awash in a . . . Rain of Fear!

Editor: Christopher Harbo
Designer: Kayla Rossow

Printed in the United States of America.
PA49

TABLE OF CONTENTS

Hidden in the shadows,
a hero keeps watch.
He is the Caped Crusader
against crime. He is the
Dark Knight of justice.
These are …

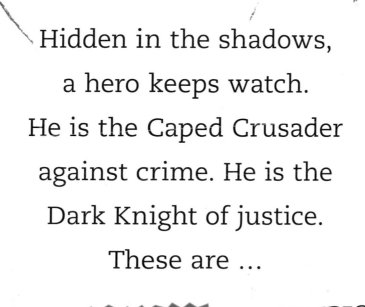

The AMAZING ADVENTURES of
BATMAN™

Chapter 1

A STORM BREWS

On a moonlit night, the
Bat-Signal brings Batman
and Robin to Gotham City.
They find the Scarecrow
and his minions running
wild through the streets.

The Dynamic Duo chases
the Scarecrow into the
Gotham City Observatory.

"End of the road,
Scarecrow," Batman says.

It's a trap! The Scarecrow
uncovers a new fear cannon.

"It's the end of the road

for you, Batman,"

the Scarecrow

says with a laugh.

"I've mixed all my fear formulas together!" the villain says. Then he fires the cannon into the sky.

SHAZACK! SHABOOM!

Dark clouds swirl as a
storm erupts over Gotham
City. The Scarecrow's fear
toxin rains down.

"Uh-oh," Robin says.
"This is bad."

Robin puts on his gas mask. Batman starts to do the same, but the Scarecrow snatches it away and throws it on the ground.

SMOOSH! The villain stomps on the mask and destroys it.

"Take a deep breath, Batman," the Scarecrow growls. "Of fear!"

The toxin makes Batman see strange shadows come to life! They slowly creep toward the Dark Knight.

"Get away!" he shouts.

"Now I'm unstoppable,"

the Scarecrow cackles.

"Everyone will know the

power of fear!"

It's up to Robin to save

the city.

Chapter 2

ROBIN TO THE RESCUE

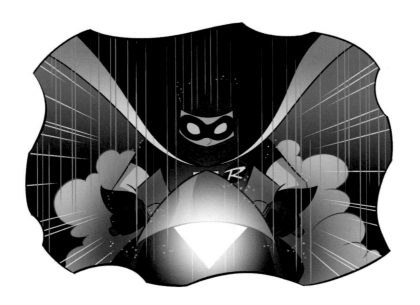

"Hang in there, Batman,"
Robin says. "I've got a plan."

The Boy Wonder hops on
his Redbird motorcycle and
zooms away!

"Not so fast, little bird," the Scarecrow shouts. Then his minions toss pitchforks to block Robin's escape.

"You won't catch me!" Robin says, swerving around the roadblocks.

As Robin escapes, he
sees people shaking with
fear. He wants to help them,
but he knows he must get to
the Batcave first.

When Robin arrives at
the Batcave, he runs to the
laboratory. He combines all of
Batman's fear gas antidotes.

PLOOP! FIZZ!

"This should protect

Batman from the fear toxin,"

Robin says.

"But how will

I save the rest

of the city?"

Chapter 3
FINAL SHOWDOWN

CRACK-A-THOOM!

The toxic storms grow

stronger. Fear spreads

through Gotham City. Time

is running out as Robin races

to save Batman.

The Scarecrow's minions

form a human chain across

the road. Robin knows he

can't break through.

VROOM! VROOM!

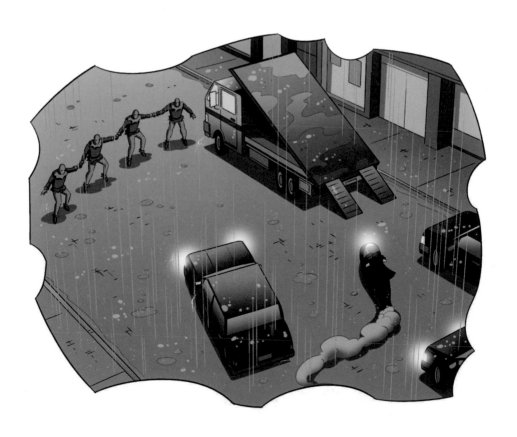

The hero zooms up a tow truck bed. He jumps over the chain of minions!

"Yahoo!" he shouts, flying through the air. Robin lands safely and hits the gas again.

Meanwhile, the fear toxin

makes Batman think the

shadows are attacking him!

"You're not going to win,

Scarecrow," Batman says.

"Robin will stop you."

The Boy Wonder dashes

into the observatory.

"Get him!" the Scarecrow

tells his minions.

THWACK! Robin trips

them with his staff.

"You won't get by me!"
the Scarecrow shouts,
jabbing his pitchfork. But
Robin slides under his legs!
He trips the villain and
dashes toward the cannon.

Robin places the antidote inside the Scarecrow's fear cannon. "I hope this works," he says.

SHABOOM!

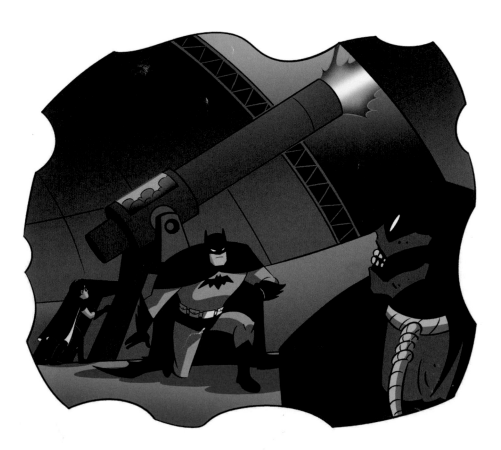

The cannon fires the antidote high into the sky. It spreads across Gotham City.

At last, the storm of fear clears! Gotham City returns to normal.

The Scarecrow scrambles across the floor and darts for the door. Batman tosses his bolas! They tangle around the Scarecrow's legs.

"Your rain of fear is over, Scarecrow," Batman says.

"What a day!" Robin says with a grin. "I'm ready to take a break."

Suddenly the Bat-Signal lights up the clouds again.

"On second thought," the Boy Wonder says, "looks like it's time for another amazing adventure!"

BATMAN'S SECRET MESSAGE!

Hey, kids! What is the Scarecrow's real name?

10 15 14 1 20 8 1 14

3 18 1 14 5

Use the code below to solve the Batcomputer's secret message!

1	2	3	4	5	6	7	8	9	10	11	12	13
A	B	C	D	E	F	G	H	I	J	K	L	M

14	15	16	17	18	19	20	21	22	23	24	25	26
N	O	P	Q	R	S	T	U	V	W	X	Y	Z

antidote (AN-ti-dote)—something that stops a poison from working

bola (BOW-la)—a weapon made of several balls connected to a rope that is thrown to entangle prey

formula (FOR-myuh-luh)—a mixture of chemicals used to change something

laboratory (LAB-ruh-tor-ee)—a room where scientists do experiments

minion (MIN-yun)—a follower of a powerful person

observatory (uhb-ZUR-vuh-tor-ee)—a building designed to study outer space

toxin (TOK-sin)—a poisonous substance

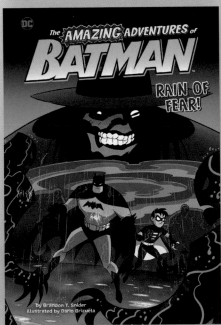
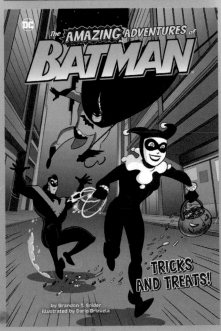

Author

Brandon T. Snider has authored more than 75 books featuring pop culture icons such as Captain Picard, Transformers, and the Muppets. Additionally, he's written books for Cartoon Network favorites such as Adventure Time, Regular Show, and Powerpuff Girls. He's best known for the top-selling *DC Comics Ultimate Character Guide* and the award-winning *Dark Knight Manual*. Brandon lives in New York City and is a member of the Writer's Guild of America.

Illustrator

Dario Brizuela was born in Buenos Aires, Argentina in 1977. He enjoys doing illustration work and character design for several companies including DC Comics, Marvel Comics, Image Comics, IDW Publishing, Titan Publishing, Hasbro, Capstone Publishers, and Disney Publishing Worldwide. Dario's work can be found in a wide range of properties including Star Wars Tales, Ben 10, DC Super Friends, Justice League Unlimited, Batman: The Brave & The Bold, Transformers, Teenage Mutant Ninja Turtles, Batman 66, Wonder Woman 77, Teen Titans Go!, Scooby Doo! Team Up, and DC Super Hero Girls.